CH

THE
SECRET
ROOM

Uri Shulevitz

Farrar   Straus   Giroux

New York

To Stephen Roxburgh

ONE DAY a king was traveling through the desert.

There he met a man.
"Why is your head gray
and your beard black?"

"Because my head is older than my beard."

The king was pleased with the man's reply.

"You must not tell this to anyone
until you have seen my face
ninety-nine times," the king ordered.

When the king returned home, he asked his chief counselor: "Why does a man's hair turn gray before his beard?"

The chief counselor didn't know why.
And he was not clever enough to figure it out.

But he was shrewd.
He asked one of the king's companions
where they had traveled.

Then he rode out into the desert and found the man.
"Why is your head gray and your beard black?"

"I cannot tell you," said the man.

"I am the king's chief counselor. If you don't tell me,
 I'll have you thrown in prison. If you do,
 I'll give you one thousand gold coins."

"Ninety-nine copper coins will do," said the man.
The chief counselor gave him the money
and got the answer.

"What a fool that man is, to have asked for so little."

When the chief counselor answered the king's
question, the king summoned the man at once.
"You have disobeyed me."
"But, your Majesty, I followed your orders," said the man.

"How so?" asked the king.

"I did not tell him until I'd seen your Majesty's face
ninety-nine times — on these coins," said the man.

The king was so impressed with the man's cleverness that he appointed him treasurer. And the man served the king diligently.

In time, the king came to value his advice in all
matters and rewarded him handsomely.

As the man's influence grew, so did the chief
counselor's envy. Day and night he thought:
I must get rid of that man.

So he accused the man of stealing gold from
the treasury and hiding it in his house.

When the king heard this,

he went to the man's house.

They searched for a long time
but found nothing.

Then the chief counselor discovered
a door that was locked.
"Aha!" he said. "A secret room!"

The king ordered the man to unlock the door.

But the room was empty.

The king was astonished.

"What is this secret room?"

"Your Majesty, I am grateful for all the honors
  and riches you have given me," said the man.

"But I must not get too full of myself.

"So I come every day to this room to remind myself
that I am still the same man with the gray head and
the black beard whom you once met in the desert."

"I knew you were clever," said the king.
"Now I know you are wise."
 He dismissed the chief counselor
 and appointed the man in his place.